DISCARD

Harry
GOES to DOG SCHOOL

Scott Menchin

Balzer + Bray
An Imprint of HarperCollins *Publishers*

Balzer + Bray is an imprint of HarperCollins Publishers.

Harry Goes to Dog School
Copyright © 2012 by Scott Menchin
All rights reserved. Manufactured in China.
No part of this book may be used or reproduced in any manner whatsoever without written
permission except in the case of brief quotations embodied in critical articles and reviews.
For information address HarperCollins Children's Books, a division of HarperCollins Publishers,
10 East 53rd Street, New York, NY 10022.
www.harpercollinschildrens.com

Library of Congress Cataloging-in-Publication Data is available.
ISBN 978-0-06-195801-4

Typography by Carla Weise
12 13 14 15 16   SCP   10 9 8 7 6 5 4 3 2 1
❖
First Edition

For Alessandra

Harry's parents wanted the best
for their boy.

There was only one problem. . . .

Harry did not want to be a boy.
He wanted to be a dog.

"Oh, look at the cute kitty."

"Time to clean up, Harry!"

"Let's clean behind your ears, Harry."

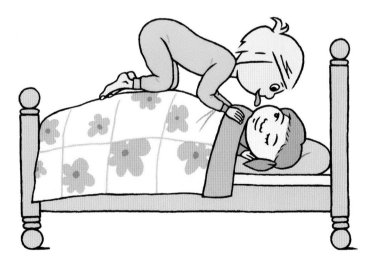

"Harry, sweetie, give your little sister a kiss good night."

There was only one thing
Harry's parents could do.
It was time to send Harry
to school.

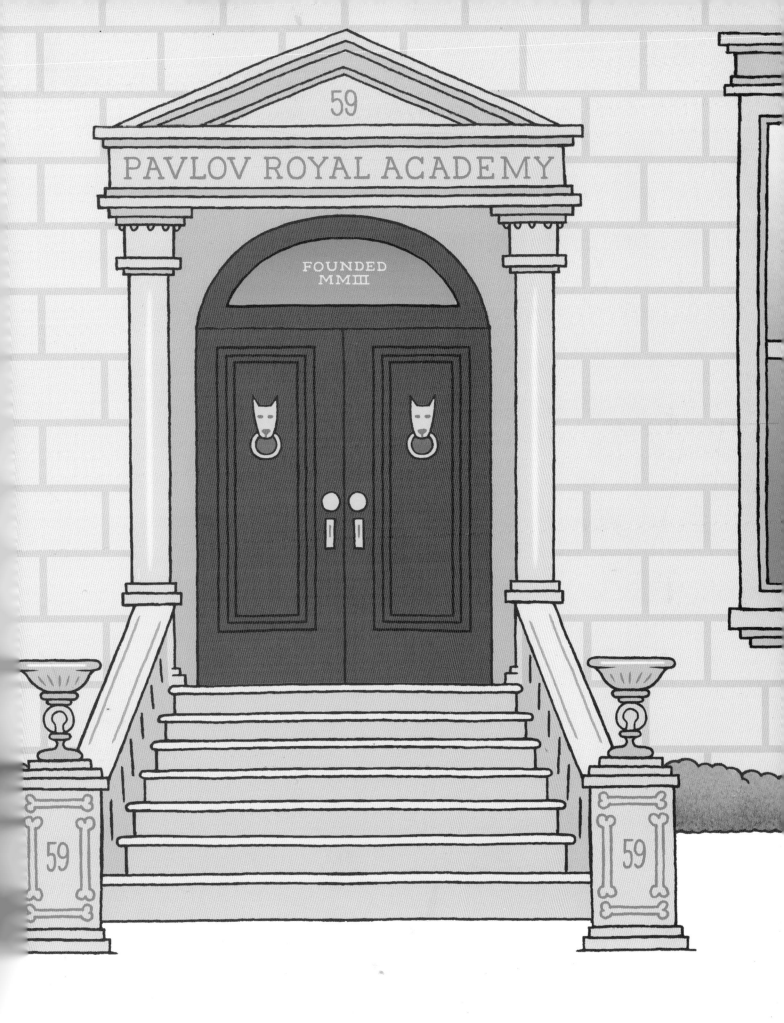

They waited to see Mr. Stockhausen,
the headmaster.

Mr. Stockhausen peered down at the boy and declared, "Harry is definitely different, but we like challenges at the Pavlov Royal Academy."

On the first day of class,
Harry met his new friends.
School was a dream come true!

The teacher, Miss Weatherwax, started with the basics.

She clapped her hands several times and said, "Listen up! Two straight rows, please."

"Ready, class? Sit!"
Harry sat.

"Roll over!"
Harry rolled.

"Fetch!"
Harry fetched.

"Good boy, Harry!"
Harry loved school.

Next was recess . . .
time to go outside and play!

The lunch bell rang.

"Come and get it!" a smiling
Miss Weatherwax announced.

Harry was starving.

But lunch was not what he expected.

After lunch, Harry took out his crayons and started drawing.

He showed his classmates his favorite superhero.

He tried getting everyone to play with building blocks.

But his new friends didn't play like he did.

"Nap time!"
Miss Weatherwax called out.

But Harry just couldn't fall asleep.

"You know, I could really use an extra pair of hands," Miss Weatherwax said. "Would you like to be my helper?"

Harry liked helping, but it was hard work.

Exhausted, Harry finally fell asleep.

He dreamed about
riding his bike . . .

playing baseball with
his friends . . .

reading to his
little sister . . .

watching his favorite
TV show . . .

eating a big bowl of
chocolate ice cream . . .

and sleeping in his very
own soft, warm bed.

At the end of the day, Harry's parents came to pick him up.

Later at dinner, Harry announced,
"I think I would like to be a boy again."

His parents were okay with that.

Now Harry goes to a new school,
where he really likes being a boy . . .

. . . most of the time.